Daisy
Takes a Ride

Kim Weybrecht

Illustrated By
Morgan Spicer

BROWN BOOKS KIDS

Daisy Takes a Ride

Brown Books Kids
Dallas, TX / New York, NY
www.BrownBooksKids.com
(972) 381-0009

A New Era in Publishing®

Publisher's Cataloging-In-Publication Data

Names: Weybrecht, Kim, author. | Spicer, Morgan, illustrator.
Title: Daisy takes a ride / Kim Weybrecht ; illustrated by Morgan Spicer.
Description: Dallas, TX ; New York, NY : Brown Books Kids, [2020] | Interest age level: 004-007. | Summary: "During a strangely sudden trip to the hospital, Daisy's owners ask her to wait in their truck until they return. But after a curious poke around the camper nearby in the parking lot, Daisy goes on an unexpected camping adventure of her own -- and comes home to an even more unexpected surprise!"--Provided by publisher.
Identifiers: ISBN 9781612544694
Subjects: LCSH: Dogs--Juvenile fiction. | Camping--Juvenile fiction. | Newborn infants--Juvenile fiction. | CYAC: Dogs-- Fiction. | Camping--Fiction. | Babies--Fiction. | LCGFT: Action and adventure fiction.
Classification: LCC PZ7.1.W4374 Da 2020 | DDC [E]--dc23

ISBN 978-1-61254-469-4
LCCN 2020908508

Printed in United States
10 9 8 7 6 5 4 3 2 1

For more information or to contact the author, please go to
www.BrownBooks.com.

DEDICATION

To my amazing husband, Jason.
Your support and love mean everything to me.

ACKNOWLEDGMENTS

I would like to thank my children, Evan and Amy, for listening to my bedtime stories and always asking for more, even when I just wanted to sleep. You are the joys of my life, and I am so proud to be your mother. Thank you, Dad, for teaching me the value of hard work. Mom, thanks for instilling a love of reading in me (even if it only took later in life!).

I would like to thank my beautiful sisters, lifelong friends and readers, for taking the time to put their books down and play with me, and my brother, who showed me what a fierce competitor looks like both in bike racing and Monopoly.

A thank-you to the wonderful Krista Hill for editing and talking me through the publishing business, to the incredibly talented Morgan Spicer for the beautiful illustrations that made Daisy come to life on the page, and to Jay Fairfield for his insight and giving me that nudge to finally get this book published.

Thanks to Thomas Reale for looking at my story before I even had a title and to the entire team at Brown Books Publishing Group for helping me put this story into little hands. I am truly grateful.

And as ever, another big thanks to my husband for his continuous positive energy. I couldn't have done this without you.

Daisy was a beagle. She lived with her loving owners, Sam and Zoe. She was an energetic dog who loved to play outside.

Daisy was brown and white. After a long day of play, she could look totally brown!

Then Zoe would give her a bath.

Zoe also took her for a walk every day. Sam and Daisy liked to play fetch. Afterward, Daisy was sure to get a treat. Her favorite treat of all was peanut butter.

One night in the wee hours, Daisy woke up. She could hear excited voices.

Sam and Zoe rushed out the front door. Sam had a suitcase.

It's too early to be leaving on vacation, thought Daisy.

She jumped in the truck with Zoe and Sam, and they sped off.

Sam was driving very fast. Zoe made strange noises.

Daisy licked Zoe's face.
She wanted to help her!

Then she heard Sam on the phone with the vet. He asked if he could bring Daisy by the kennel as soon as they opened in a few hours.

They pulled up in front of a large building. Sar
helped Zoe out of the truck.

He patted Daisy's head. "Wait here, girl," he sai
"I'll be back soon." He rolled down the windov
partway and closed the door to the truck. The
he and Zoe went inside the big building.

Daisy tried to stay awake, but she soon grew tired.
She settled on the front seat and took a nap.

When she woke, sunlight was streaming through the windows. Daisy yawned and stretched. She jumped up and looked outside for any sign of Sam and Zoe. They were nowhere to be seen. Instead, there was a large camper parked next to the truck.

Daisy was tired of being cooped up. So, she squeezed through the partway-opened window and jumped down to the ground.

She began sniffing around the camper. Its door was cracked open, so she hopped inside to look around.

She found a nice, cozy bed in the back. Daisy curled up and went to sleep once more.

She began dreaming about her favorite treat: peanut butter!
Her dream was so real she could smell it!

Daisy opened her eyes. A little girl was standing before her with
ooey peanut butter smeared all over her freckled face. Daisy
opped up and began licking the delicious peanut butter.

The girl giggled.

Then Daisy stopped. The camper was moving! She jumped up to look outside. *Oh, no!* she thought. *Sam and Zoe will think I abandoned them!*

The man driving the camper saw her. "How in the world did that DOG get in here?" he shouted.

A woman came over to Daisy and read the tag on her collar. She patted Daisy on the head. "I will call your owners, Daisy, and let them know you are safe."

"I'm Emma," the little girl told Daisy.

While the woman called Sam and Zoe,
Daisy and Emma played hide-and-seek.

The woman got off the phone. "Daisy's owners are glad we found her," she said. "They happen to live in our neighborhood. They were going to kennel her, but they asked if we wouldn't mind taking her on our camping trip, since they are going to be busy at the hospital for a few days."

"Hooray!" Emma cheered.

The family stopped at a store to buy groceries and some dog food. Emma used her jump rope as a leash for Daisy.

Soon they reached the campground. Emma and Daisy
jumped out and went for a walk. Daisy was happy to
run around the woods, sniffing all the new smells.

They found a small stream, and Daisy splashed in the cool water. A frog hopped up on her nose, and Daisy barked wildly.

That night, while Daisy cuddled next to Emma in the camper, Emma told her a bedtime story about a frog.

The next day, Daisy went with Emma to a tennis court. Emma had a can of balls and a racket. She hit the balls. Daisy chased them all over the court.

I like playing tennis! thought Daisy.

Daisy was having the time of her life on the camping trip. At night, though, when she snuggled against Emma, she would think of Zoe and Sam. She was beginning to miss her owners.

One day, the family packed up everything and drove away from the campground. Daisy rode along, wondering where they were going next.

It was a long drive with only a few breaks.

Finally, they came to a stop.

Daisy jumped out. She was home!

Daisy bounded across the yard and up the steps, barking wildly. Sam came running out the door. "We missed you, girl!" he said as he leaned down to pet her.

Zoe appeared, holding a bundle in her arms. "Daisy, this is Rose," she said.

She showed Daisy a tiny baby. She let Daisy sniff the baby's blanket. Daisy somehow knew she had to be gentle.

Sam and Zoe thanked Emma's family for caring for Daisy. They told Emma she could come over and play with Daisy anytime. Daisy wagged her tail happily when she heard that!

After Emma's family left, Daisy followed Sam and Zoe into the house. She watched as Zoe put Rose down for a nap.

Daisy was happy to be back with her own family. She couldn't wait for little Rose to grow big enough that they could run and play together.

And, thought Daisy,

*I hope she likes
peanut butter!*

About the Author

Kim Weybrecht grew up in the Midwest, the second eldest of five children. Camping and biking adventures were a huge part of her family's lifestyle. One of her first jobs was as a summer park counselor, where she played games and told stories to children.

Throughout her career, Kim has taught, tutored, and coached children. As a volunteer school librarian, she loved reading to kids and encouraging them to get excited about books.

Today, when Kim isn't with kids, she enjoys playing tennis, running, and baking muffins. She and her husband share their home in Highland Heights, Ohio, with two teenagers and a boisterous beagle.

About the Illustrator

Morgan Spicer has illustrated more than thirty picture books. Since founding her small business, Bark Point Studio, in 2012, she has been lucky enough to draw thousands of dogs, cats, and other animals from all over the world. A friend to all animals, Morgan donates art and a percentage of all sales to animal rescues, which is really what it's all about!

Morgan Spicer lives a happy, vegan life in the woods by the sea with her husband and four rescue dogs.